Mr. Dogwood goes to Washington

by

Leigh Anne Florence

Illustrations by James Asher

Cover design and book layout by Asher Graphics
Illustrations by James Asher

Manufactured in the United States of America

All book order correspondence should be addressed to:

HotDiggetyDog Press
P.O. Box 747
Shepherdsville, KY 40165

502-376-5966
leighanne@thewoodybooks.com
www.thewoodybooks.com

Dedication

*This book is proudly dedicated to the members of our
United States Armed Forces.*

*Whether you are presently serving or whether you are a veteran,
we thank you for protecting and defending the great
United States of America.*

Foreword

As I read to my daughters about Woody's and Chloe's adventure to Washington D.C., it reminded me of my first trip to our Nation's capitol as a young boy. I was an Army brat and our family had just returned from a four-year tour overseas and our country was preparing for the Bicentennial, celebrating our Nation's 200th birthday. As I stood on the lawn in the middle of the Mall on a beautiful blue day, I was enormously impressed at the spectacular site of the Capitol in one direction and the Washington Monument in the other. Even more than the impressive architecture of these historic buildings and monuments was the realization of what they stood for, freedom. It was one of the moments in your life you never forget.

During this visit, our parents took us to Arlington National Cemetery. On entering this hallowed and sacred ground, I realized there was a connection between the Nation preparing for its' 200th birthday and the thousands of American heroes laid to rest in the immaculately maintained cemetery. Even as a young boy, I understood that the freedoms our countrymen enjoy was not by accident. It was secured by the sacrifice of fellow Americans fighting for the idea of freedom. We respectfully stood quietly admiring the precision and military discipline of the Soldiers guarding the Tomb of the Unknowns. I read the inscription on the tomb, "Here Rests In Honored Glory An American Soldier Known But To God." It was an emotional event. My mind was full of thoughts of the Soldiers in that Tomb and of the Soldiers they represented. These Soldiers would never again enjoy being with their family on a bright blue beautiful day as I was.

I returned to our Capitol twenty-five years later with my own family, my wife and two daughters. I was now a Soldier like my father. Like my earlier visit, it was a bright blue day during the Labor Day weekend of 2001. My daughters were now experiencing what I did as a boy. Little did we know that 10 days later our nation would be attacked and our freedoms threatened.

During my combat deployments overseas, my daughters enjoyed reading about the adventures of Woody and Chloe. We have had a life-long love of dachshunds with my boyhood dog, Artie, and our current dog, Dino. The stories of Woody and Chloe comforted our daughters by keeping their mind off the stress of having a parent deployed.

I think it is important that all Americans make a trip to our Nation's capitol. If you can't do it in person, then you can through Woody and Chloe in their latest adventure in *Mr. Dogwood Goes to Washington*. In our fast-paced lives, it is important to take time to reflect on what makes this all possible. I have seen societies where freedom was under daily assault and I realize we should never take our freedoms for granted. In *Mr. Dogwood Goes to Washington*—in a fun, informative and respectful way— our children can experience the significance of visiting our capitol through the adventures of Woody and Chloe. It is a trip worth taking.

Christopher Hickey
Colonel, U.S. Army
Fort Leavenworth, Kansas

Woody would like to thank...

Mom, Dad, and Chloe – You are the best family in the world. The day you rescued me was the best day of my life! I am one lucky dog!

Lynne – I can't imagine doing my job without you! Who would handle my schedule and phone calls? You are the best Chief of Staff any wiener dog could ask for!

The WOODY TEAM –Sue, Nathan, Shaun, and Lori - Thanks for doing the "Behind the Scenes" work so Chloe and I can shine!

Sunshine Pack and Ship – Nobody can pack and ship like you! Thanks Lynne, Alan, and Janice for making sure our books end up at the right place!

James Asher, our illustrator – What more can we say? Even my Washington Monument masterpiece can't compare with your talent! A special thanks to Kris, your granddaughter, for her time and patience!

The great ladies at McClanahan Publishing – Paula, Michelle, and Jo. We always love the finished product!

Kriss Johnson – Newspapers in Education Manager – We make a PAWS-atively perfect team! Thanks for all your help and guidance. More importantly, thanks for being our dear friend!

David Thompson and everyone at the Kentucky Press Association – We are so thankful for this incredible opportunity. We hope we always make you proud! (No, Chloe still can't live with you!)

Lexington Herald-Leader Marketing Department – Bekki, Jennifer, Steve, Kathy, and Kevin – You are like family! Thanks for always making us feel welcome when we visit the fourth floor!

Scott and Kat Johnson – You are our voice! Thanks for bringing us alive!

The Collins Family and the Hickey Family – especially Amanda, Julia, and Dino for making the book extra special.

Wanda Klingensmith, Ellen Stites, and all the students and teachers at Holiday Elementary in Hopkinsville for all the emails and letters!

Louisville Gas & Electric/Kentucky Utilities – E.ON U.S. – especially Cliff Feltham, Chip Keeling, and Chris Hermann as well as Kentucky Secretary of State Trey Grayson – This story would not be possible without your help.

The 88 Kentucky newspapers, editors, and all the schools who participated in the newspaper series – Thanks for traveling along with us on our journey.

Finally, to our founding fathers (and founding mothers), our military troops (past and present), our government leaders, and all the men, women, and children who have sacrificed to make our country the great nation that it is! I am so proud to be an American.

Chapter 1

I can't believe I'm in the doghouse again! Well, not my real doghouse, but my personal time-out corner I sit in when foolishness gets the best of me! You would think I'd learn to follow the rules, but many times my mischievous ways overtake sensible thinking. When that happens, I hear my full name, find myself in the corner, and head to bed without dessert!

Where are my manners? Let me introduce myself. My name is Dogwood, but everyone calls me Woody. I'm an eight-year-old black and tan miniature dachshund (or wiener dog) from Kentucky (Making me "Woody, The Kentucky Wiener!"). Being the runt of the litter or underdog, the owner of that Kentucky tobacco farm said I wouldn't amount to anything. That all changed the morning a lady and her one-year old redheaded miniature dachshund appeared. The lady scooped me up and we instantly fell in love. Mom and the other wiener dog (Chloe, who's now my sister) took me outside, gave me a name, and the rest, as they say, is history!

Our family has grown to include Dad (a human), two brothers (Rio, a Labrador, and Little Bit, a cat) and two sisters (Cheyenne, another Labrador, and Dolly, another cat). Even though there is plenty of barking, meowing, chasing and fetching, there's also work to do. We call it teamwork!

You see, Mom writes books about us. Not only did people read the books, but also my phone started ringing. "Woody, can you come to our school and talk about dreams, goals and hard work?" As an underdog, I knew about those things. Dad always says we can achieve, with hard work. "It doesn't matter that you're little," Dad says, "it's your attitude and work ethic that count, so work and dream like a big dog!" While Mom, Dad, Chloe and I travel to schools, our siblings watch over the home place, keeping the lions, tigers and bears at bay! (We've never seen a lion, tiger, or bear in the neighborhood!)

In fact, we've been so busy that we haven't taken a vacation in years. Imagine our surprise when Dad said he was treating Mom, Chloe and me to a vacation! "Where?" Chloe and I barked. "Washington D.C. – our nation's capitol!" Dad replied. We were PAWS-atively thrilled! We've been planning our route, packing our Scooby suitcase, and counting the days before we head east!

Dad bought us a coloring book of D.C. It has pictures of well-known monuments. Everyone knows how much Chloe and I love to color, so we've been spending our free time coloring the stately buildings, trying our best to stay between the lines. Dad was sure the book would help us prepare for our trip. What he didn't count on was that my love of art would land me in the doghouse! Mom told us we couldn't play until we picked up our toys and brushed our teeth. "Then you can have free time," Mom said. "And Woody, no more coloring

until you've completed your chores!" "Yes Ma'am!" I answered, fully intending to obey, but what would it hurt if I finished my masterpiece? "Just a few more minutes and then I'll start my chores," I thought.

Chloe was minding Mom, explaining that I better obey too, yet I was sure Mom would understand once she saw my stunning portrayal of the Washington Monument. Wrong! What Mom saw was scattered toys and food stuck between my teeth from lunch. The next thing I knew, Mom called me Dogwood and ordered me to obey at once. She didn't have to tell me twice! Once I accomplished the task, Mom scooped me up, just like she did that spring day eight years earlier, and gave me a kiss. "I love you, Woody. You're a sweet little boy, but you must follow rules! You know what this means, don't you? You must sit in the corner and think about your actions - and no dessert either." After a few more hugs, kisses, and tears (sniff, sniff), I found my way to my familiar corner.

So, here I am, realizing I've been selfish. My parents are taking Chloe and me on dream vacation – Washington D.C. - and I can't even mind my manners. I can't wait until Mom returns so I can tell her again how sorry I am. While I'm waiting, I think I'll close my eyes (yawn) and imagine the Capital City. See what happens next time when our paws hit the ground in D.C. Will we meet the President? I'll keep you posted. In the meantime, remember to obey your parents and Work and Dream like a Big Dog!

Chapter 2

When we crossed the Potomac River and saw the Washington Monument surrounded by the colorful cherry blossoms, I felt a lump in my throat!

Hi, fellow Americans! Let me start at the beginning. Mom, Dad, Chloe and I bid farewell to our brothers and sisters, climbed in our dependable, old Woody Bus and left our Shepherdsville, Kentucky home early this morning to travel east to our nation's capital.

We had only gone about, oh, three miles before I said, "Are we there yet?" Chloe and Mom smirked, but Dad didn't think it was all that funny. "Woody, this is going to be a long trip, the longest you have ever taken. It will be at least eight hours before we get there – nine if we have to stop every hour just so you can eat. Please don't ask every five miles if we are there yet – and please don't tell me how hungry you are. You just ate!"

I was thankful I hadn't opened my big mouth to express my concern over my rumbling tummy and was even more thankful for my stash of Scooby snacks. I knew my favorite picture books would keep me occupied, not to mention coloring in my favorite Washington D.C. coloring book, but eight

hours was a long time! "I've got it!" said Chloe. "How about we sing some patriotic songs?" "That's a terrific idea!" I said, clearing my throat. "I love to sing. What's a patriotic song?" Everyone laughed, and then Chloe explained that a patriotic song is about our country. "You know, Woody, like *The Star Spangled Banner* or *You're a Grand Old Flag!*" My sister is so smart! So, as we journeyed along, we sang, *This Land is Your Land, God Bless America* and *America the Beautiful.* Mom taught us songs about Johnny marching home, the land of cotton called Dixie, and my new favorite about the Yankee with a feather in his cap. (That song makes me giggle every time!)

The time flew by! Before I knew it, we were crossing over the Potomac River! I had colored the Potomac in my coloring book. I had learned that it was called the "Nation's River" because it travels through our nation's capital. Mom said that George Washington spent lots of time around the Potomac. In fact, George Washington chose the location of the nation's capital because of the Potomac, and because at the time it was in the center of the country! Mom also told us that Washington, D.C. gets its name from George Washington, our country's first president, and D.C. stands for the District of Columbia. Dad said that it was originally called Federal City or Washington City before it became Washington D.C. Today, many people call our nation's capital "The District" or simply "D.C." since they don't want to confuse it with the state of Washington. We also learned that D.C. is located between Virginia and Maryland. In fact, part of the District is in Virginia, the other part Maryland. While Dad was driving,

Chloe and I were soaking up all the information Mom was giving us. "Wow!" My mommy sounded like an official Washington D.C. tour guide! I always knew my mommy was the smartest mommy in the world, but how did she learn all of that information? "It's amazing what you learn when you spend time reading, Woody!" Mom said. (I made a mental note to self to read more books!) "Besides, while you and Chloe have been working in your coloring books, I have been researching and learning as many facts as possible so I could pass the information on to you!" I really did have the greatest parents in the world!

It was amazing how much I had already learned, and to think we hadn't even gotten out of the Woody Bus! It was then Dad suggested we stop and eat dinner, find a hotel room and get a good night's sleep. "We have many things to see and do while we're here," Dad said. "You will want to be rested when we start sightseeing tomorrow!" I didn't feel tired at all. I guess it was all the excitement.

With those instructions, I better say goodnight. Chloe and I are so excited. We can't wait to hit the streets of our Capital City! Where will we go first? Will it be the Capitol, the Lincoln Memorial, or the White House? So many decisions, so until next time, Work and Dream like a Big Dog!

Chapter 3

It's our first day in Washington D.C. and Chloe and I are ecstatic! I was checking my list to confirm I had everything. We've been ready for hours, but Mom made us eat a hearty breakfast so we'd have plenty of energy. While finishing our vittles, Dad asked what we wanted to see first.

"Let's go to the mall." Chloe said. "The mall?" I asked. "Chloe, are you joking? We drove all this way to see the most fantastic monuments in the world and you want to go to the mall?" I replied in my most serious voice, confident my parents would agree. When I saw their smiles, I felt the 'Open mouth, insert paw' feeling. "I'm not talking about a shopping mall," Chloe said, "but the National Mall - the open-area national park in the middle of the district where many of the museums and memorials are located." "That's more like it," I replied, slurping down the last drop of orange juice and strapping on my Scooby backpack. "What are we waiting for?"

Prancing along, I was amazed at the stately buildings. They had columns, etching, and some even had words inscribed. They were more beautiful than the pictures I had seen or colored. Looking at the street signs and checking my map, I realized we were on Constitution Avenue. The first place that caught my eye was the National Archives building. I didn't know what archives were, but I snapped a photo of the majestic structure. Dad explained that archives were a collection of historical documents. Honestly, old papers didn't sound

exciting, but Dad promised we would enjoy it, and would learn much needed information. "Besides Woody," Dad continued, "our trip will be more meaningful if you understand America's history."

We noticed many people looking around and whispering. We saw guards in uniforms standing erect and helpers at the front desk giving information. Mom picked up a brochure and began reading. She explained the National Archives protects the records of the government. It also displays the original documents known as the Charters of Freedom like the U.S. Constitution, the Bill of Rights, and the Declaration of Independence. I was confused. "Bill of Rights? Constitution?" I had so many questions. A guard must have noticed my confusion because he approached and asked my name. "I'm Woo- I mean, uh um, Dogwood and this is my sister, Chloe." I also explained this was our first time in D.C. I then lowered my head and confessed I didn't know much about the making of America. He invited us on a tour of the Archives and promised to explain things and help me become more civic-minded. I didn't know what being civic-minded was, but I was relieved I would soon find out.

"Before we look around, let me give you a brief history lesson," the nice gentleman said. "In 1775, Great Britain ruled America. The colonists (people living in America's 13 colonies) were angry because they didn't have rights. They had to follow the rules of the British king. When the king said 'Pay more taxes!' the Americans said 'No Way!' so the colonists and the British began to fight. The colonists realized they needed to declare their freedom from Great Britain, so in June and July of 1776, the colonists chose some men to help with declaring their freedom. Thomas Jefferson wrote what we call the Declaration of Independence. Benjamin Franklin and John

20

Adams assisted him, among others. The declaration stated that everyone had the right to life, liberty, and the pursuit of happiness. So, on July 4 of 1776, representatives of the 13 colonies approved the declaration and the United States was born. After this, America still had to fight many years to be free, but the declaration was the first step." I was silent. "Wow!" I finally said. "I thought there had always been a United States. I didn't know men and women had to work to make America." The guard smiled and said, "Dogwood, you have no idea!"

Finally, the gentleman asked if the four of us would like to see the Declaration of Independence. "It's here?" I asked. "It's right here. Follow me," the guard said. I couldn't believe it. This had to be a dream come true!

So, fellow Americans, we're on our way to see an important piece of history. I have to concentrate, so it's goodbye for now. In the meantime, Work and Dream like a Big Dog!

Chapter 4

Hi, fellow Americans! I'm standing in the National Archives building reading the actual Declaration of Independence – the document that stated that all men were created equal and granted us rights. It's amazing to see a document that was written more than 230 years ago! When the guard at the archives asked whether I wanted to see the actual declaration, I was excited and scared that clumsy little me would even be near such an important piece of history. I was relieved to see it was enclosed in a glass case. In fact, I saw many cases that contained documents. The guard, who had become our unofficial tour guide said, "Come on. I'll show you what's in the others."

"This is the Constitution of the United States. Remember when I told you the Declaration of Independence gave birth to America in 1776, but we still had to fight for freedom? Well, the Constitution, written by our "founding fathers," developed a federal government. The Constitution said the U.S. was a republic – meaning citizens had rights. It also said the U.S. would have a president who is elected by the people. In addition, there would be a Congress to make laws, a Supreme Court (the highest court in the land) to uphold the laws, and a system among the three of those branches to "check and balance," so no branch would gain too much power." I imagined what it would be like to actually write the Constitution. I still struggled writing my full name; I could only dream of handwriting a piece of history.

After seeing the Constitution, I thanked the guard, thinking we had seen all there was to see. "Wait, pups! You can't leave now! I haven't shown you the Bill of Rights!" "Bill who?" I asked. "The Bill of Rights," he answered, "the document that gives us freedom. After the Constitution was written, a government was in place but the rights of citizens had not been addressed. So, amendments – or changes – were made to the Constitution. The first ten changes are called The Bill of Rights, and it gives us freedoms."

"Freedom from what?" I asked. "Well," the guard continued, "the first amendment says we have freedom of speech, religion, press, and assembly." "In wiener dog terms, please," I said. He smiled and said, "It means you can express your opinion – either by barking or writing – without fear of being punished. Freedom of press means that people who write or broadcast news can tell what's happening in the world. Freedom of religion means we can follow any religion – or not follow any religion – without being punished; and freedom of assembly tells citizens that we can join any group or political party without government involvement. The first amendment also says that we can ask the government to help if we feel we've been punished unfairly."

Wow! After hearing about our Bill of Rights, I felt so –

well, FREE! I didn't know citizens had so many rights. I wondered whether Chloe and I had any rights as wiener dogs. Did we have the right to chase the kitty cats in our neighborhood or to bark at the mailman? I was pondering those questions when the guard handed me a brochure with the Bill of Rights listed. I made a resolution to learn all ten amendments. I was certain that would help me be more civic-minded, even if they didn't apply so much to wiener dogs. The four of us thanked the guard and headed to the National Mall.

I was thinking about my rights when I saw the longest two words I had ever seen. I was sounding out the letters when Mom chimed in and said, "Look, the Smithsonian Institution!"

We learned the Smithsonian Institution is the world's largest museum with 19 museums and galleries. It could have taken days to see just one Smithsonian. Chloe's favorite was the Museum of American History. She loved seeing the dresses of the First Ladies, Abraham Lincoln's hat and even Mr. Roger's sweater! My favorite was the National Air and Space Museum. I pretended I was an Apollo astrodog. How cool to be the first dog to walk on the moon. I can hear it now, "Houston, The Wiener Dog has landed!"

Next time, see if I am orbiting the earth. In the meantime, Houston, Work and Dream like a Big Dog!"

Chapter 5

Wow! I can see the Lincoln Memorial, the Jefferson Memorial, the Capitol, and even the White House!!!"

Hi, fellow Americans! I'm in a slice of heaven known as the National Mall. It's unbelievable, all the buildings, memorials, and monuments that are located in the central area of D.C. known as the Mall. After hours in the Smithsonian, and landing from my walk on the moon, we left the Smithsonian Museums in search of some notable monuments. Everyone knew how I had been excited to see the monuments and memorials. I had been working in my Washington, D.C. coloring book and I wanted to see how my artistic effort compared. The Jefferson Memorial was our first stop. Before our visit to the National Archives, I really didn't know much about Thomas Jefferson. As a founding father, the third president of the United States, and the author of the Declaration of Independence, it was clear why he had a memorial all his own. It was beautiful. The dome-shaped rotunda, the statue of Jefferson, and passages from the declaration gave me goose bumps!

We were on our way to another monument when Dad

suggested we stop for a picnic on the grassy area of the Mall. Funny, I wasn't tired, but I didn't say no to food. As Mom was handing out the sandwiches she had packed, she asked me a question. "Woody, when the man at the National Archives asked you your name, why did you say 'Dogwood'?" I knew someone in my family would notice, so I tried to explain. "Well, Woody is fine for my family and friends to call me when we're home in Kentucky, but I figured since we were in our nation's capital, I needed to sound more serious, more dignified." "I don't understand," Mom said. "Everyone in D.C. has such serious names," I said. "It's Thomas – not Tommy Jefferson. Benjamin – not Benji Franklin. George – not Georgie Washington. I'm just a little-bitty, small-town, ordinary wiener dog —not a big-time, intelligent politician. I didn't want anyone to laugh at me!" Mom picked me up and gave me a kiss. "Finish your sandwich. I want to show you something," Mom said. In a flash, we were at yet another memorial.

"This," Mom said, "is the Lincoln Memorial, dedicated to our 16th president." Many believe he was our greatest president. He led the nation through the Civil War, gave memorable speeches such as his Gettysburg Address, and freed the slaves. And you know what, Dogwood?" Mom asked. "Mr. Lincoln was just a small-town, ordinary country boy from Kentucky. He was born in a log cabin on his father's farm and didn't have much money, but he educated himself to become a lawyer and politician. Everyone called him "Honest Abe" since he was known for his character and integrity. I bet he was never ashamed of his name, his birthplace, or even his size. In fact, most of our founding fathers were ordinary men from all over, doing extraordinary things." Mom and I smiled at each other as I soaked in what she had said. "How about we visit the Washington Monument, Dogwood?" "Sounds great!" I replied. "And Mom, please call me Woody!"

Before I could turn around, we were standing at the base of the Washington Monument. Out of all the monuments in my coloring book, this was a favorite, though I didn't know exactly why. Maybe because it paid tribute to our country's first president. It might have been the 50 flags – one representing each state – around the base, or maybe because it was so tall! Dad suggested we take the elevator to the top. It didn't take long for the four of us to reach the top of the tallest structure in D.C. Looking out of the 555-foot building, Chloe and I were amazed at all we saw. We could see memorials we had just visited as well as get a view of the Capitol and White House. I was amazed that I didn't even need my Snoopy binoculars. It was clear as a bell! I also was beginning to realize that so many men like Washington and Jefferson had sacrificed so much for my freedom! I couldn't get enough of learning about our country!

"Dad, I can't wait any longer! We must go to the Capitol and the White House!" "Let's go!" Dad replied. I can't wait to tell you what happens! In the meantime, Work and Dream like a Big Dog!

Chapter 6

Hi, fellow Americans! We didn't think anything could be better than the Archives, Smithsonian, or monuments, yet the Capitol Building was just as impressive! Chloe and I were thrilled to learn we could tour the Capitol. Like other buildings in Washington, we went through security before entering.

The guards searched my backpack before smiling and saying, "Enjoy." We listened as our guide gave us information about the Capitol. Located in the center of D.C., the Capitol is where Congress makes laws. "There are three main areas of the Capitol," the tour guide explained. "The Senate chamber, the House chamber and the Great Rotunda – the area under the dome where ceremonies are held. Any questions?" My heart fluttered. Mom always said there weren't any dumb questions, so I raised my paw. "My name is Dogw... I mean, Woody, and I wondered what the Senate and the House of Representatives do?" I thought I heard some snickers, but was glad when the guide said, "Great question, Woody! Congress is divided into two parts – the Senate and the House of Representatives. They make laws (rules) for our country. To make it easier Woody, let me give you an example. Think of a

law you would like to see passed." "Hmmm…" I thought. "Well, Chloe and I wish for a law against eating hot dogs!" Snickers turned to laughter, but the guide continued. "Let's pretend the 'No Eating Hot Dogs' Bill is introduced in the Senate. The Senate debates and votes. Members of both the House and Senate meet and re-write parts of the bill that are not in agreement. Then, they both vote on the bill. If it passes in both chambers, it goes to the President of the United States. He can sign the bill, making it a law, not sign, or veto the bill. Even if he vetoes the bill, there's still a chance it could be passed and you would get your 'No Eating Hot Dogs' law."

I was thinking about the Hot Dog bill when we arrived on the third floor of the Capitol. "Here we can watch Congress," informed the guide. I was amazed as I looked down and saw people actually making our laws. "Why is that person banging a hammer?" The guide explained it was called a gavel, which was struck at the beginning and ending of a session, or to call order. Maybe I could be in charge of the gavel when I grew up. That would be a dream job!

I was still thinking about my gavel career as we exited the Capitol and were inside the U.S. Botanic Garden and saw more than 4,000 plants. "Woody, these are not trees in our back yard, if you know what I mean. Keep all fours on the ground at all times!" Dad didn't have to explain that twice, though I was now sorry I had drunk so much Jungle Juice earlier. Mom and Dad must have been worried because we didn't stay there long.

While still on the Capitol grounds, I saw a gentleman

and a very pretty lady I had seen on television. They were waving at everyone and had some Scottish Terriers with them. I barked, but they didn't hear me. "Hey! Arff! Over here!" I exclaimed! I thought I heard Mom and Dad telling me to hush, but I had to get their attention. Without thinking, I took off across the Capitol lawn, running and barking with all my might. I had almost reached the Terriers when two men in dark suits and sunglasses swept me off my feet. "Rut row," I said, borrowing a Scooby phrase. I could tell they weren't happy. The man who was holding me asked for my ID. I was thankful I had my library card. Shaking, I handed the card to the gentleman. Since I wasn't supposed to talk to strangers, I felt I should know their names, so I quietly and respectfully asked. "We're the Secret Service," he answered. "Secret Service?" I repeated. "I love secrets! You can tell me! I won't tell anybody!" The two men looked at me and I knew I was in deep trouble. "We're not in the business of telling secrets, son. Our job is to protect the President of the United States and you just posed a threat. Let's find your parents."

Oh no! The trip had gone so well – a dream come true, yet this was a nightmare and I was praying I would wake up! I don't know what's going to happen, but I know it's not going to be good. I have a feeling the doghouse is in my immediate future. Keep your fingers crossed for me and Work and Dream like a Big Dog!

Chapter 7

Hi, fellow Americans! It's Chloe. It's probably no surprise that my brother is in the doghouse. When Woody saw the Scottish Terriers at the Capitol, he had to say hello! Being the friendly little guy he is, he meant no harm. He was surprised when two men in suits stopped him in his tracks. They introduced themselves as the Secret Service and explained their job was to protect the President and his family. They searched Woody's backpack, questioned him and then returned him to Mom and Dad. You could tell by the look on Woody's face that he was so relieved to be back with his family. Woody apologized to everyone and explained that he just wanted to say "Arff" to his fellow canines. The Secret Service accepted his apology. They explained they would not formally punish Woody, but instructed him to always pay attention to the rules. Woody thanked the men and apologized once again. The men left and Woody began to cry. (Don't tell him I told you!) We hugged Woody and told him we loved him, and then Mom and Dad told Woody he would have to pay the consequences. He must memorize *The Pledge of Allegiance* and *The Star-Spangled Banner*. I told Woody I'd let everyone know he was okay and that the incident had not landed him in jail!

Though I was sorry Woody was in trouble, I was happy to share what I've learned while visiting Washington D.C. I had learned so much about our founding fathers, but what about our founding mothers? Being a girl, I knew there must be some ladies that helped shape America. I asked Mom, confident she would know. She gave me information on many exciting women. I learned about Martha Washington – the *first* First Lady of the United States. I also learned about Abigail Adams. Like Mrs. Barbara Bush, Mrs. Adams was the wife of one President and the mother of another. I loved reading about Dolley Madison, the wife of James Madison. According to history, Mrs. Madison was very pretty and very smart. During the War of 1812, she was planning a dinner party when the British invaded D.C. She had to leave the White House, but not before she packed up a painting of George Washington, the Declaration of Independence, and her pet parrot! My favorite story though was about Betsy Ross. Legend has it that Betsy Ross sewed the first official American flag. According to Mrs. Ross, three men – one of whom was George Washington – came to her house one day in 1776 and asked her to sew the very first American flag. (George Washington was not yet the President, but a General in the Army.) Betsy knew George Washington since they attended the same church. In addition, she had sewn ruffles on his shirts. Therefore, he knew she was a great seamstress. General Washington showed Betsy a design of a six-point star. History says that Betsy took her scissors and cut a five-point star in one single snip. Amazed, the men

changed the design from a six-point to five-point star and gave her the job! The first flag had 13 white stars on a field of blue and 13 red and white stripes – 13 representing the colonies. Since then, the flag has changed to include 50 stars – one for each state, yet the 13 stripes remained unchanged.

I love seeing the American flag fly in schools, public buildings and even our own front yard. Mom and Dad have always taught us that every time we see the flag we should remember our freedom and be thankful that we live in the greatest country of all! Because it represents America, Mom says we always need to treat it with respect by not letting it touch the ground, not letting it stay in the rain, and even standing to salute it during *The Star Spangled Banner* and *The Pledge of Allegiance.*

I was inspired. Girls could do important things, too! I realized everyone's job is equally significant. I also realized I wanted to learn to sew. (This could be tough since Mom never lets us use sharp scissors.) I was thrilled when she said she would give me some sewing tips. Who knows? Maybe I'll sew something that makes the fashion magazines. So, my friends, goodbye for now. Mom is waiting with a spool of thread! Hopefully Woody will be out of the doghouse next week! In the meantime, take a minute to observe the flag and be thankful for our freedom – and, in the words of my brother, "Work and Dream like a Big Dog!"

Chapter 8

Freedom of speech, freedom of press, and for me, freedom from the doghouse! Hi, fellow Americans! Boy, is it great to be out of the doghouse. I've done some silly things in my life, but running on private property without permission was at the top of my "Worst Mistakes" list. The Secret Service agents were forgiving. Mom and Dad were, too. They reminded me that when we make poor choices, everyone suffers. The Secret Service agents had to chase me down and catch me, the Scottish Terriers and their parents had to be whisked off to safety in case "the barking wiener dog posed a risk," and rumor has it that Homeland Security was being contacted. (I'm not sure what that meant, but it wasn't good.) In addition, Chloe had to bail me out by writing to you, all the consequences of my mistake. Mom says that's one way we learn from our mistakes. So, Mom and Dad made me write and memorize *The Pledge of Allegiance* and *The Star Spangled Banner*. Funny, it didn't feel like punishment at all. After completing my assignment, Dad asked me whether I understood what The Pledge really meant. "Not really," I confessed. Dad said he would try to explain it by breaking it down into small parts.

" 'I pledge allegiance' means that we're promising to be

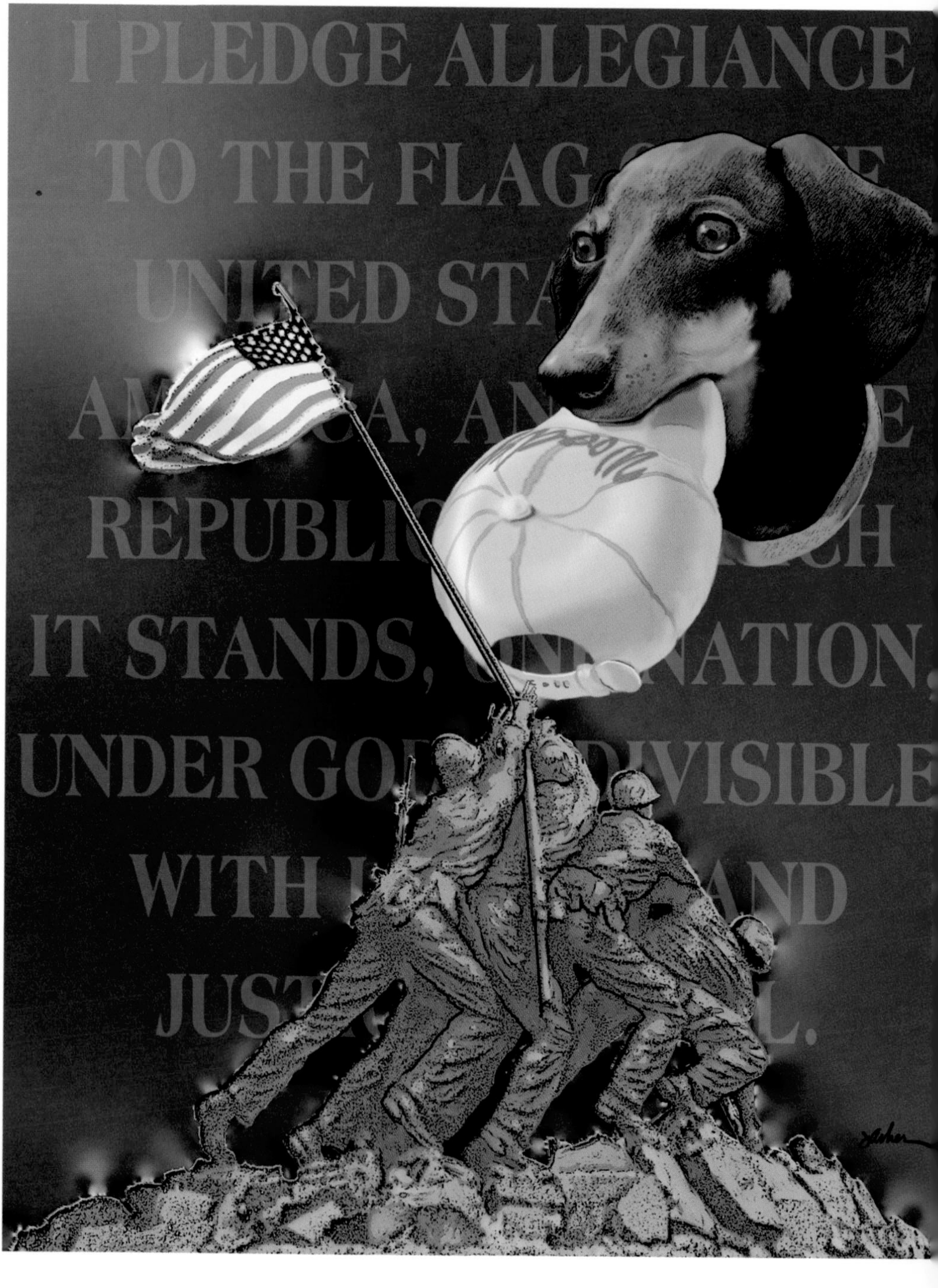
I PLEDGE ALLEGIANCE
TO THE FLAG
IT STANDS,
NATION,
AND

loyal to something," Dad said. "In this case, to our flag – which symbolizes America and freedom. 'To the Republic' reminds us that our country is made up of people." Dad asked if I understood before he continued. " 'One nation, under God, indivisible' means we are a united country and we aren't going to let anybody tear us apart. 'With liberty and justice' means we have rights and freedoms, and 'for all' means just that – it is for everyone." I said The Pledge a few more times and tried to soak it in. I stood up, faced the American flag, took off my cap, put my paw over my heart, and recited the words. I realized I was promising to be loyal to my country and do my best to be a good citizen. I still wasn't 100% sure what being a good citizen really meant, but since the government gave me rights and freedoms, I had the duty to be the best citizen that I could be. Many people – such as our hard-working military – had sacrificed too much for me to take freedom for granted. I remembered in the back of my coloring book was a page that included five tips on being a good citizen – or member of our country. I pulled out my coloring book and read the suggestions.

Show everyone you love your country. I definitely loved America and realized I could demonstrate that love by singing the National Anthem, respecting the flag and the other symbols of this country.

Obey the rules of authority. I had just learned this lesson the hard way. "It means obeying the law, as well as the rules of your parents and teachers," Dad explained.

Help your community. Hmmm…like giving to others, volunteering, like the humane society, and not littering.

40

Treat others with respect. "Remember Woody," Dad said. "We have to treat everyone with kindness no matter their age, their background, their size, or their color."

Work hard, pay taxes and vote! As a wiener dog, I was having trouble with this one. Dad explained that we must work to make money and help the country run. "Paying taxes is a law. Taxes help run the country. They help pay for roads, schools, libraries, and even humane societies. As far as voting, it is the process in which we elect our president, governor and other officials." "Will I ever vote?" I asked. "No, Woody. In order to vote, you must be 18 years old and a human! But even though you can't vote, you can be a good citizen by learning about the candidates and their beliefs."

I was thinking of other ways to be more civic-minded when Dad told me to gather my things. He said he was taking mom, Chloe and me to a place that would surely help me understand the meaning of freedom and citizenship. I can't imagine where, but I can't wait to tell you about it. In the meantime, show your love to America; obey the laws and Work and Dream like a Big Dog!

41

Chapter 9

Hi, fellow Americans! It is a gorgeous day and I have never been more proud to be an American. You see, Mom, Dad, Chloe and I are standing in Arlington National Cemetery. As with the other places in Washington, D.C., Arlington National Cemetery has a Visitor's Center that offered maps and guidebooks. Chloe and I knew from previous places that the brochures helped us learn lots of information. We sat on a bench outside the cemetery reading the facts about this historical burial place. Mom and Dad explained that we needed to remain quiet and respectful while on the grounds of the cemetery. We needed to read the information and ask our questions before we entered.

Arlington is located in Arlington, Virginia – just outside of D.C. – across from the Potomac River. More than 600 acres, it's the burial place of more than 300,000 servicemen and women from all of our nation's wars, as well as other famous Americans such as President Taft and President Kennedy. "What's a serviceman?" I asked. Dad explained that a serviceman or woman was anybody who was in the military or armed forces. "It would be someone in the Army, Navy, Air Force, Marines and Coast Guard. They protect our country.

Remember when the colonists had to fight to gain freedom from Britain? Well, the colonists realized they needed a military to protect them. That is when the first military was started." Dad went on to tell us that today there are about 500,000 servicemen and women stationed all around the world protecting our freedom.

"Puppies," Mom said. "Do you realize that every single person buried in this cemetery paid the price for our freedom? They actually gave their lives and died so that we could live in the greatest country on earth." For once, I was at a loss for words. I couldn't imagine that somebody loved me enough to fight for my rights and freedoms. Sure, my parents and siblings loved me, but they knew me! These soldiers didn't even know my name, yet they cared enough about our country and me to dedicate their lives to America. "One more thing before we enter the cemetery," Dad said. "Pay special attention to the Tomb of the Unknowns." I opened my mouth to ask, but was glad when Chloe beat me to the question. "I don't understand, Daddy. What is the Tomb of the Unknowns?" she asked. Dad explained that it is a monument in the cemetery dedicated to the American soldiers who died without their remains being identified. That is when I saw Chloe's first tear.

We quietly entered Arlington to pay our respects. We walked along, not saying a word to each other, though I was sure we were all thinking the very same thing – that living in America was a privilege. As we approached the Tomb of the Unknowns I saw guards protecting the tomb. Dad had explained earlier that the tomb is guarded 24 hours, seven days a week, no matter the weather. As we approached, we saw the words inscribed on the tombstone.

Here Rests In

Honored Glory

An American

Soldier

Known But To God

As we left the cemetery, I felt an American pride I had never felt before. Once we were outside the cemetery, Chloe and I promised each other that the next time we saw a military person, we were going to stop and say thanks. "See Woody," Dad said, "Already you are thinking like a true patriot!" I smiled!

Leaving the cemetery, I felt the need to go home. Maybe it was the somberness in my heart from Arlington. I couldn't put my paw on it. I didn't feel tired, even after all we had seen. Fact is, I didn't even know how long we had been gone, but I asked Dad when we would be returning to Kentucky. "Before we head back to the Bluegrass state," Dad said, "There is one more very important place we have to visit."

One more place? Where could it be? I can't wait to find out. In the meantime, thank a military person, and Work and Dream like a Big Dog!

Chapter 10

Hi fellow Americans! I must be dreaming! I'm actually here - 1600 Pennsylvania Avenue where the most famous house in the country is located! That's right! I'm at the White House!

After leaving Arlington National Cemetery, I had the strange feeling we needed to go home. "Woody, remember when you chased after the man and woman with the Scottish Terriers?" Dad asked. "Remember? I've been trying to forget that entire incident!" I answered. "Well," Dad continued, "That just happened to be the President of the United States!" I couldn't believe it! Dad went on to tell me that the President and First Lady were walking on the Capitol lawn with their pups. "The pups you chased were the First Dogs of America!" Dad said. "Oh no!" I thought. "That explains the Secret Service." "Dad, we must get out of here! Once the President realizes who I am, I'll be kicked out of the White House and into the doghouse again!" Mom, Dad and Chloe all laughed! "Relax, Woody," Dad instructed. "The President realized you meant no harm and invited us here so you could make a formal introduction. The Secret Service told us to wait outside and the President will be right out! And Woody, this time please wait!"

My heart was pounding. I was thankful I had put on my bow tie and combed my hair! I had no idea I would meet the President today! What would I say to him? I didn't want to say anything silly or embarrass myself, but I had to think quickly about how I could express my appreciation. I wanted to thank him for leading our country, for protecting us from harm, and for keeping America great. My time had run out because I saw a shadow coming toward me. It was getting closer, and closer...

"Woody?"

"Yes?" I replied.

"Woody?" the voice said again.

It was weird. I heard my name, but all of the sudden I felt terribly confused.

"Woody, son, wake up. Honey, you've been asleep a long time!"

I was puzzled. One minute I'm at the White House, the next minute I'm in the corner of the bedroom at home. I checked for my bow tie. It wasn't there!

"Wake up, son," mom said one more time.

"Mom, wait. Where's the President?" I asked. "The President?" she repeated.

"You must have been dreaming, Woody," Mom said. "Remember, you were punished for coloring in your Washington, D.C. book when you should have been doing chores so I put you in the corner? You must have gone to sleep."

"Oh, Mom! What about the Washington Monument and the Declaration of Independence? Are you and Dad still mad about the 'Secret Service' incident?" Mom laughed. "I don't know what you're talking about, Woody, but it's okay now. You aren't at the White House, but the white house you call home — the one in Kentucky — and you're safe with us!" Mom picked me up and kissed me. "It's time for dinner. Besides, tomorrow will be an exciting day. We'll be leaving early for our vacation to Washington, D.C. You and Chloe will want to be rested and ready."

I couldn't believe it! It was a dream! It felt like a dream — at one point even a nightmare — but it was so incredibly real! I was shocked at how many things I had learned in my sleep. Even in my dreams, I had learned about the history of our country. I had learned about our founding fathers — and mothers — who helped shape America. I had learned what it meant to be patriotic and civic-minded. I learned we have military men and women who sacrifice their lives to keep us free; and I learned to never, ever run on private property again! Most of all, I learned the words of my favorite patriotic songs were true, "There ain't no doubt, I love this land. God Bless the U.S.A!"

So, fellow Americans, I'll say goodbye for now. Mom, Dad and Chloe are calling me for dinner. We have an exciting day ahead. I can't wait to cross the Potomac, view the Washington Monument, and pay respects to the soldiers at Arlington. Since I can't eat dessert tonight, maybe Mom will let me color a few more pictures in my favorite coloring book. By the way, keep your eyes open. You never know when I might show up, maybe even in your back yard. In the meantime, love your country with all your heart, be thankful for your freedom, and as always, Work and Dream like a Big Dog!

Woody, a.k.a. Mr. Dogwood

50

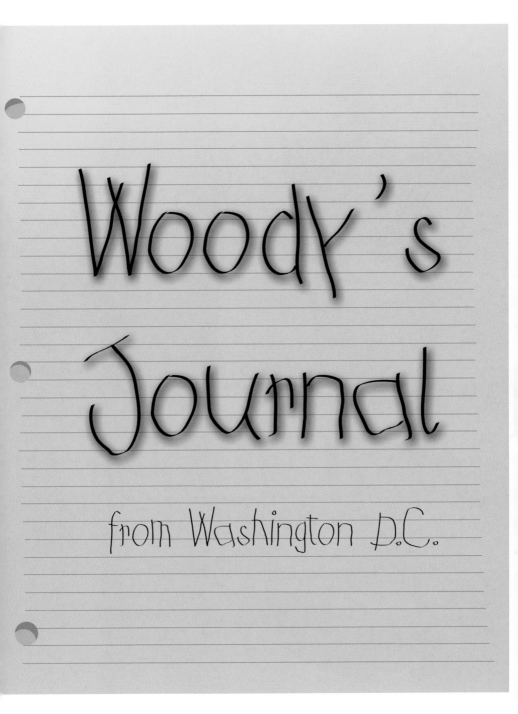

Woody's Journal

from Washington D.C.

Favorite Spots at the Mall

(National Mall — NOT Shopping Mall)

Washington Monument

Lincoln Memorial

United States Capitol

Smithsonian's Air and Space Museum

Thomas Jefferson Memorial

Favorite First Dogs in History

Fala   President Franklin D. Roosevelt's dog

Fido   President Abraham Lincoln's dog

Veto   President James Garfield's dog

Pete   President Theodore Roosevelt's dog

Barney and Miss Beazley

President George W. Bush's dog

Favorite Patriotic Songs to Sing

Yankee Doodle

You're a Grand Old Flag

This Land is My Land

God Bless the U.S.A.

The Star Spangled Banner

Yankee Doodle

Written by Richard Shuckburgh in the early 1750's

Yankee Doodle went to town
A riding on a pony
Stuck a feather in his hat
And called it macaroni.
Yankee Doodle, keep it up
Yankee Doodle dandy
Mind the music and the step
And with the girls be handy.
Father and I went down to camp
Along with Captain Gooding
And there we saw the men and boys
As thick as hasty pudding.
Yankee Doodle, keep it up
Yankee Doodle dandy
Mind the music and the step
And with the girls be handy
There was Captain Washington
Upon a slapping stallion
A giving orders to his men
I guess there was a million.
Yankee Doodle, keep it up
Yankee Doodle dandy
Mind the music and the step
And with the girls be handy

The Pledge of Allegiance

Written by Francis Bellamy in 1892

Adapted by Congress in 1954 to the way we say it today

I pledge allegiance to the flag

of the United States of America

and to the republic for which it stands,

one nation under God,

indivisible, with liberty and justice for all.